The Complete Works of Gottfried Keller
Volume II

CW01498027

NEWCOMB LIVRARIA
·PRESS·

Mixed Thoughts about Switzerland

Gottfried Keller

Translation with Afterword by
Tim Newcomb

Contents

Mixed thoughts about Switzerland

It would not be entirely inappropriate for us young Swiss, at a time when people have begun to deny our nationality, when they want to force us mentally to love our fatherland not as a Helvetic one, but as a German, a French, an Italian one, when every insipid, lumpen journalist of foreign countries takes the liberty of talking rubbish about Switzerland which testifies to nothing but the ignorance of the Swiss, where every Kaffir newspaper ridicules Switzerland and its internal institutions, when at such a time we sometimes turn our thoughts to this fatherland and try to order our feelings in the great struggle of principles that is moving Europe at the present time; To this end, I take the liberty of entertaining you today with a few intemperate ideas and reflections, on the condition, however, that I give them merely as my individual views and invite anyone of a different opinion to express his or her counter-opinion in suitable submissions as well; in this way, our weekly journal will gain in interest and many who otherwise do not contribute much to the entertainment of society will be forced to contribute their mite. Above all, we turn our attention to the recent attacks of Germany against our nationality. I hope there will be no one among us who would have been in the least confused about this point, although in Germany one seems to be generally convinced of the infallible correctness of these unfounded assertions. The Germans believe that they can silence us mainly by asserting that the Swiss people do not belong together at all according to their ancestry, but that German Switzerland actually belongs to Germany, French Switzerland to France, etc., in short that each part of our country belongs to that part of the bordering states which corresponds to its ancestry, and this is deliberate disregard of our national character. For, granted that we are descended from the same tribes of peoples as our neighbors, this does not matter at all. The spirit of generations changes infinitely, and if we had to follow that view and the Bible, the whole of mankind would be only one nation, and consequently would have to constitute only one state. The present population of England has arisen from Britons, Romans, Anglo-Saxons, Normans, Celts, etc., all of whom have alternately conquered, displaced, or oppressed each other, and yet the English nation is now a whole, indivisible, original in character, and not similar to the present French, Germans, or any people. It is the same with the Swiss. The original cantons have always been free in their mountains; no lord is known to have ever ruled them by law. Albrecht sought to force them, and from then on they created their own destiny, and to this gradually, until our times, the whole of present-day Switzerland has been attached, partly out of inner urge and inclination, partly out of outward necessity; and through the constitutions they gave themselves they have become just as different from those with whom they had common descent. The national character of the Swiss does not consist in the oldest ancestors, nor in the legend of the country, nor in anything else material; but it consists in their love of freedom, of independence, it consists in their extraordinary attachment to the small but beautiful and expensive fatherland, it consists in their homesickness, which afflicts them in foreign countries, even the most beautiful ones. If a foreigner loves the Swiss state institution, if he feels happier with us than in a monarchical state, if he joyfully enters into our customs and naturalizes in general, then he is as good a Swiss as one whose fathers already fought at Sempach. And conversely, if a Swiss sympathizes too much with France or Germany, if he finds himself comfortable and happy as the subject of some foreign sovereign, if he adopts foreign customs out of inclination and despises native customs, he is no longer a Swiss, he is a Frenchman, an Easterner, wherever his heart draws him, and this cannot always be imputed to him as a sin; for man's inclinations and desires are as many as the stars in the sky. While Schiller sings with all the ardor of his heart the fiery words: "Man is created free, is free, and was he born in chains!", the Privy Councillor of Goethe lets his Tasso say in noble comfort: "Man is not born to be free, and for the noble there is no greater happiness than to serve a prince whom he loves."

If the two greatest writers of our time spoke such different words, how can one blame more limited mortals if one seeks his true home there, the other there. But what a man has once felt to be true, he should stick to; what he has recognized as his spiritual and material happiness, from that he should not leave until he gets another conviction. Now the Swiss has once found that the independence of the entire fatherland, the freedom of thought and word, the complete equality of rights and non-validity of class and other externalities is the need of his soul. But he would have to renounce all this by joining other tribes formerly related to him, according to the present conditions of the state; or he would have to assert his principle and seek to extend it, and that is not in the nature of a true Swiss. For this has always been the most beautiful virtue of our Confederation, that it does not, like France, seek to proselytize everywhere, but is content in itself, and it was the most prosperous times of Switzerland, it was most respected, when it was strong in the simplicity of its old customs and in the disregard of foreign commerce. The Swiss likes to speak of his freedom, but he does not seek to impose it on anyone, and why should he not speak of it with love; after all, every good subject likes to speak of his king just as much, and our king is once freedom, we have no other. May it always be the true, the undoubted freedom; but this has always been the substance of the internal quarrels of our country, that it was sought and fiercely denied by one part in this form, by the other in that. Some think they see it only in the aristocratic, others in the democratic constitution, and the latter, while they think they possess the truth, are again led astray by a caste which should be high above both parties; I mean the clergy. There have been republics where aristocracy was more suitable for the welfare of the people than democracy; only those aristocrats loved their people, respected them and recognized their true profession. The same cannot be said of ours. The present remnants and followers of the patricians in most cantons, especially in Zurich and Basle, are selfish, money-grubbing, dirty, braided, they do not love the people, seek to hold the helm only out of private interests and imperiousness, are often immersed in the most mindless philistinism, and completely lack that finer education and higher culture of the mind which otherwise so distinguished the aristocrats of other republics; In short, what should be their main characteristic, they are not noble. There are some very honorable exceptions to this, but they are so few that they make no impression among the masses. Although I do not know any of the sovereigns now living whose subjects I would like to be, there have been those whose rule I would rather have endured than that of our governments in the 17th and 18th centuries, the time of the spiritual and spiritualistic revolution. The heartless and spiritless regents put the light under a bushel and sat on it, the stiff braid in the neck; where their wives and daughters turned the possessions of the so-called peasants and tradesmen into silk and damask clothes and cheekily boogied in them; where the priests were the best alchemists, knowing how to turn the sweat of the people into vain gold, which they hung in heavy chains around the ever-thirsty throat and put in thick rings on the greedy fingers. But this time, thanks be to him who hates the night and loves the day, has long since passed; it has lain like an oppressive nightmare on the hearts of the people, but they have stirred and taken fresh breath and opened their eyes to the eternal light that shone into the land. It cannot yet tolerate this light everywhere, although it is not a new one, for our fathers have already seen it; but it will become accustomed to it again when it drives away the shy race of night birds that flutter around the light and try to extinguish it.

The time has come when the spiritual elements of our country are engaged in the fiercest struggle. They are almost hostile to each other, and among their representatives we see capable men on both sides, but also on both sides many mere muzzlers. We will probably live to see the crisis; let us indulge in the beautiful hope that every honest Swiss will see his true salvation fulfilled in it. But only he is entitled to this hope who does not lack anything in himself that can benefit the whole, who impartially and incorruptibly considers the usefulness of every opinion quietly for himself and, if it has proved itself good, accepts it, whether it comes from an aristocrat or a democrat, whether it fits into his previous system or not. Now, however, we cannot deny to ourselves that even on our liberal and radical side not everything has always been so. Our radicals are often as harsh, as blinded, as intolerant as only an inveterate aristocrat can be. The love of freedom has not infrequently degenerated into thoughtless shouting, religious freedom of thought has become a cold mockery and denial of every religious principle and an insolent mockery of all that is holy. There are only a few who can be accused of this, but sadly, they are the most talented minds. Likewise, it has been too little considered that not everything new has become good, not everything old has become unfit and bad. While one gives more and more nourishment to the spirit and brightens up the heads, one not infrequently lets the heart grow cold. One has become too prosaic in many things. These include, above all, the complete neglect of the fine sciences and arts and the abrupt separation from foreign countries; for in this respect Germany is far ahead of us, and it does our political nationality no harm at all if we take as a model the foreign countries that are superior in art and literature. Only by accepting every good thought, from whom it may come, by appreciating the truth in every party, by hating in our opponents not the person but only the false principles, and by carrying reconciliation in our hearts even during the most heated struggle, by gladly acknowledging without all conceit that the citizen of other states can also be happy, by never stifling the divine spark of eternity in our breast and never losing our sacred trust in the one who guides the stars: Only in this way can we look forward calmly and with composure to the sunrise of the only truth; it will perhaps rise blood-red, this sun; the firns and ice caps of our free fatherland will perhaps glow in gloomy purple, but the crystal-bright day will nevertheless dawn and spread its happy, pure blue over our silver mountains.

Afterword by the Translator

Keller is nearly completely unknown outside of Switzerland, but his literary legacy still leaves a mark on the art of the 20th century. The trajectory of Gottfried Keller's life and artistic evolution is marked by a series of transformative experiences. His academic journey was disrupted due to a youthful prank, leading to his departure from higher education and the subsequent pursuit of training as a landscape painter. After completing a two-year period of study in Munich, he returned to his hometown bereft of financial resources in 1842. It was during this period that he underwent a notable transition, influenced by the political poetry prevalent in the pre-March era, which ignited his poetic sensibilities and concurrently drew him into the militant movement catalyzing Switzerland's reconfiguration in 1848.

Keller's intellectual pursuits then led him to Heidelberg through a travel scholarship provided by the Zurich government. Engaging with the intellectual milieu of Ruprecht-Karls University, he embarked on studies encompassing history and political science including the writings of the former Heidelbergian, Ludwig Feuerbach.

Subsequently relocating to Berlin, he intended to embrace a trajectory as a playwright, however, his creative inclination saw a divergence towards the composition of novels and novellas. Among his notable achievements are "Der grüne Heinrich" and "Die Leute von Seldwyla," emblematic works that garnered prominence. Upon his return to Zurich in 1855, his reentry was marked by both recognition as a writer and persistent financial constraints, a situation ameliorated in 1861 upon his appointment as the First State Secretary of the Canton of Zurich. His narrative oeuvre included "Fähnlein der sieben Aufrechten," which encapsulated a dual expression of contentment with national conditions and a circumspect contemplation of societal progress-associated perils. He was a life-long reader of Marx's favorite philosopher (next to Hegel), Feuerbach, which laid the philosophic foundation of his Atheism.

Keller's foray into political responsibilities spanned a decade, within which his creative output was partially subdued, only witnessing a resurgence during the latter phase of his administrative tenure, yielding creations such as "Die Sieben Legenden" and the second part of "Die Leute von Seldwyla."

Goethean Prose and Legacy of Romanticism

The landscape of Swiss-German literature would be incomplete without the monumental contributions of Gottfried Keller, a figure whose impact on literature and sociopolitical thought continues to resonate. Keller's art is remembered for vivid realism, remarkable narrative structures, and socio-political commentary on the Swiss Confederacy and the shifting European landscape. His work is deeply rooted in the Romantic German literary tradition of which Schiller and Goethe, his contemporaries, often examined the complexities of human nature and societal structures.

Keller's work navigates various subjects and stylistic tropes but carries an underlying thread of social commentary. His narrative often reflects the structural forces that shape human behavior and the manifestation of societal norms. This is particularly notable in his realist masterpiece, "Die Leute von Seldwyla," where Keller explores the human condition within specific socio-political constraints. The protagonists in Keller's works, often caught in a web of societal expectations and personal aspirations, reflect the common man's struggle. This narrative technique demonstrates Keller's comprehension of the human condition as shaped by both internal and external structures, a theme consistent across his oeuvre. It's not the characters who primarily drive the plot; instead, the external societal structure dictates their behavior and destiny.

Goethe and Schiller's Shadow

Johann Wolfgang von Goethe, broadly considered the greatest German prose writer of all time, was a contemporary of Keller, and Keller worked in his shadow. Keller famously noted in a letter to his friend Jakob Pferdmenges, "In my youth, I learned from Goethe that a person can do and must do what he wants, but not always when he wants" (Briefe von Gottfried Keller, 1890). This belief seems to have influenced his depiction of characters who were often caught in a struggle between personal desires and societal obligations.

Keller was important enough of a Poet at the time to be known to Goethe and Schiller, although there is no known interaction between them. Keller commented frequently upon their works in his own, and in a letter to Goethe dated October 2, 1797, Friedrich Schiller mentions Keller's elegies: "Meyer himself can probably give you more information about the author of the elegies, which you will not dislike. His name is Keller; he is a Swiss, from Zurich as I believe, and is staying in Rome as an artist. These elegies were sent to me by a Mr. Horner from Zurich. Perhaps you have already met the latter yourself; he has also already contributed something to the Horen."

Hermann Hesse was a fan of his contemporary aross the border, writing:

Among these poems are extraordinarily beautiful ones, of which one cannot comprehend that they could lie there unnoticed and unprinted for decades! But Keller's poetry is little known at all; it is rougher and more idiosyncratic than his prose. This could be seen recently at the first performances of Lebendig begraben; Othmar Schoeck wrote a sublime music for this cycle of poems, but the majority of the audience did not know these magnificent poems and sat facing them, embarrassed and shaking their heads. Perhaps it is the same with these youth poems unearthed by Fränkel. But it would be a pity.

Swiss Confederacy Politics of the 18th Century

To better understand Keller's literary approach, one must delve into the structural forces within his narratives. His storylines are intertwined with the sociopolitical climate of the 19th century Swiss Confederacy. This was a time of significant upheaval, with the forces of industrialization, nationalism, and capitalism at play. These external forces, which shaped the characters' lives in his novels, underscore Keller's belief in societal structures' prevailing influence on individual choices and actions.

Keller's narratives display a keen understanding of the Swiss society of his time, reflecting his detailed observation and critical examination of social, political, and cultural norms. His realistic portrayals were not devoid of optimism and often hinted at the possibility of societal improvement. He stated, "The present is a time of struggle; it forces us to use all of our talents and strengths to tackle the problems of the day".

In "Der grüne Heinrich," Keller's semi-autobiographical work, the protagonist's life trajectory is predominantly influenced by external circumstances and societal expectations. While the story is driven by personal reflections and introspections, it consistently highlights the societal structures and political undercurrents impacting the protagonist's life. Keller's vision of society as a complex, interdependent structure influencing individual lives underscores the importance of social constructs in defining personal identities.

The characters in Keller's works, subject to these larger socio-political structures, serve as a mirror to the human condition. They exhibit the capacity for critical thought and resistance against societal norms, signifying the potential for change within rigid systems. This is evident in "Die Leute von Seldwyla," where characters often act contrary to societal expectations, suggesting the potential for personal agency within the confines of structural forces.

Keller's Societal Critique

Friedrich Nietzsche praises Keller's work in his writing:

> "The treasure of German prose. - If one disregards Goethe's writings and especially Goethe's conversations with Eckermann, the best German book there is: what actually remains of German prose literature that deserves to be read again and again? Lichtenberg's aphorisms, the first book of Jung-Stilling's Lebensgeschichte, Adalbert Stifter's Nachsommer and Gottfried Keller's Leute von Seldwyla, - and that will be the end of it for the time being."

Keller's contribution extends beyond mere storytelling to societal critique. His novels provide a nuanced critique of the capitalist system, highlighting its influence on human behavior and societal norms. Keller portrays a society where personal relations and human values are often subordinated to economic interests, a critique that resonates with contemporary societal issues.

His contemporaries respected Keller's ability to create profound literary works that reflected the changing societal landscape. Theodor Fontane, a noted German novelist, wrote, "Keller's tales are what German literature has produced of the very best in the domain of narrative" (Briefwechsel zwischen Theodor Fontane und Gottfried Keller, 1898). Keller was admired not only for his storytelling but also for his philosophical and political insights. However, he also faced criticism from those who saw his realism as a form of pessimism or cynicism.

Remarks on Keller's poems can also be found in writings by recent German philosophers, such as Theodor W. Adorno. In the last weeks of his life, Ludwig Wittgenstein liked to read from Keller's Zurich novellas to visitors.

Keller's novel The Public Detractors was circulated under the table in inner emigration and resistance circles during the Nazi dictatorship and played a role at a meeting of the

"White Rose" in 1942; and in 1952 it was set to music by Kurt Hessenberg.

Keller and the Continentals

Keller's work has often been overshadowed by his contemporaries, such as Nietzsche and Schopenhauer philosophically, and the poetry of Goethe and Schiller. Philosophers like Arthur Schopenhauer, though not directly connected to Keller, contributed to the philosophical atmosphere that supported the shift toward realistic portrayals of human experiences. His work contained elements of realism, romanticism, and naturalism, embodying a unique synthesis of these philosophies.

Keller's work continues to resonate today because of its enduring relevance. His critique of societal norms, exploration of human nature, and optimism about societal progress are themes that remain pertinent. Moreover, Keller's commitment to realism, despite its perceived pessimism, continues to influence contemporary literature. Ernst Bloch, a Marxist philosopher, noted, "Keller was a realist who believed in the possibility of a better future. He understood that progress required an honest examination of the present" (Principle of Hope, 1959). The importance of Keller's philosophy lies in its relevance to a broad range of disciplines, including literature, sociology, politics, and philosophy.

Swiss Legacy

In 1964, as part of their 100-year celebration, Swiss Reinsurance (Swiss Re) erected a monument for Gottfried Keller, created by Otto Charles Bänninger. The choice was made because Keller, as the State Secretary of the Canton of Zurich in 1864, had signed Swiss Re's founding documents. The monument was placed in the Zürich Enge area, facing their business premises. Consequently, some sources, such as the Zürcher NZZ, noted during the monument's unveiling that Swiss Re was essentially building a monument to itself, using Keller as a means to promote their company. The uniqueness of the Gottfried Keller monument lies in the fact that it was created during a time when constructing monuments for individuals was not common anymore. By the 1960s, various memorials for Keller were already present in Zurich, including a bust in the city hall since 1892 commemorating his role as State Secretary, plaques on different buildings where he lived and worked, and the Gottfried Keller Street. Interestingly, Keller's monuments were primarily dedicated to his political activities rather than his contributions as one of Switzerland's most renowned writers. The monument itself is crafted from Istrian limestone and consists of a block representing a book, inscribed with his works, along with a larger-than-life head placed on a pedestal and a bench nearby.

Tim Newcomb
Stuttgart, Germany
Autumn 2023

Timeline of Keller's Life and Works

1819: Gottfried Keller's Birth and Early Years

Gottfried Keller is born on July 19, 1819, in Zurich, Switzerland. Keller's childhood is marked by his exposure to literature and the arts, fostering his early interest in writing.

1839: University Studies and Literary Pursuits

Keller enrolls at the University of Zurich to study literature and philosophy. During this time, the works of German Romantic writers like Goethe and Schiller, as well as the philosophy of Hegel, influence his literary development.

1846: "Poems" Publication and European Revolutions

Keller's collection of poems, "Gedichte," is published, showcasing his early lyrical talents. Europe experiences a series of revolutions, with widespread political and social upheaval, which influences the themes of many writers, including Keller.

1850: "The Green Henry" and Realism

Keller publishes his novel "Der grüne Heinrich" (Green Henry), a semi-autobiographical work that reflects the struggles of a young man growing up in Zurich. This novel is influenced by the emerging literary movement of Realism, emphasizing authentic depictions of everyday life.

1855: Move to Berlin and "A Village Romeo and Juliet"

Keller moves to Berlin, where he works as a literary critic and continues his writing. During this time, he develops the novella "Romeo und Julia auf dem Dorfe" (A Village Romeo and Juliet), a tragic love story set in a rural Swiss village.

1860s: European Literary Connections and Developments

Keller interacts with other European writers like Victor Hugo and Ivan Turgenev, exchanging literary ideas and experiences. The works of Charles Dickens and Gustave Flaubert, among others, influence Keller's narrative techniques and exploration of social issues.

1871: "Seven Legends" and Late Works

Keller publishes "Sieben Legenden" (Seven Legends), a collection of poetic and narrative pieces blending folklore, history, and allegory. In his later years, Keller focuses on shorter prose works and reflective essays that explore existential and philosophical themes.

1881: Nobel Prize Nomination and Recognition

Keller is nominated for the Nobel Prize in Literature due to his contributions to Swiss literature. Although he does not win the prize, his legacy as a significant literary figure is firmly established.

1890: Death

Gottfried Keller passes away on July 15, 1890, in Zurich, leaving behind a lasting impact on Swiss and European literature. His works continue to be studied, appreciated, and celebrated for their realistic portrayals of human nature and society.

Index of Works

1840-1842: Letters of Gottfried Keller

This collection of letters offers a rare glimpse into the thoughts and experiences of Gottfried Keller during a pivotal period in his life. Through these intimate correspondences, readers delve into the mind of the emerging writer, witnessing the formation of his literary ideas and his engagement with contemporary intellectual currents. This epistolary treasure not only sheds light on Keller's personal journey but also provides valuable insights into the intellectual and artistic milieu of the time, making it a vital resource for scholars and enthusiasts seeking a deeper understanding of Keller's early development.

1841: Mixed Thoughts about Switzerland (Vermischte Gedanken über die Schweiz)

Gottfried Keller here delves into various aspects of Switzerland, exploring its culture, society, and political landscape. Through incisive analysis, Keller examines the intersections between tradition and modernity, offering readers a nuanced perspective on his homeland. As a commentary on the societal shifts of his era, this work stands as a testament to Keller's keen observational skills and his commitment to dissecting the complexities of Swiss identity within a changing Europe.

1849: Romanticism and the Present (Die Romantik und die Gegenwart)

Keller's exploration of the Romantic movement and its relevance to the contemporary moment illuminates his intellectual depth and engagement with philosophical currents. Through a meticulous examination of Romanticism's influence on literature and culture, Keller provides a bridge between the past and the present, offering readers a sophisticated analysis of the lasting impact of this artistic movement. His insights into the tension between tradition and innovation, rooted in Romantic ideals, make this work an essential read for those interested in the evolution of artistic thought.

1861: At the MythStone (Am Mythenstein)

This is a philosophical essay related to the Mythenstein, also called the Schillerstein, which is a natural rock made into a monument to Schiller, located in seelisberg, Switzerland, and standing around 80 feet tall. It is only accessible by boat. The monument had a large inauguration ceremony in 1859, called the Schiller Festival, which Keller attended. It celebrated his greatest story, Wilhelm Tell, which Keller refers to as merely "Tell". Schiller's daughter read his poetry at the proceedings, and Keller describes the event in detail.

"Schiller never saw Switzerland in the flesh; but all the more certainly his spirit will walk over the sunny slopes and ride with the storm through the rocky gorges, even after the Mythenstein will finally have long weathered and crumbled."

1862: Day of Prayer Mandates (Bettagsmandate)

Among Keller's various official duties as the State Chancellery at the Zürcherische Freitagszeitung was the drafting of the "Bettagsmandate" (day of prayer mandates). The first of these documents was created in 1862. The government had reservations about publishing it. Keller, who himself abstained from religious ceremonies, had initially wished for well-attended church services for the Day of Prayer, but added, "However, let even the citizen who is not of a religious disposition not spend this day in restless diversion using his freedom of conscience, but demonstrate his respect for the fatherland in quiet contemplation." Many clergymen would have found it burdensome to read these words of a Feuerbachian from the pulpit, leading the government to order a more diplomatically formulated mandate from another writer.

1878: The Christmas Party in the Asylum (Die Weihnachtsfeier im Irrenhaus)

Dr. Gottfried Keller's address of appreciation for Professor Dr. Hitzig at Burghölzli at a Christmas party as he was appointed director of the Burghölzli asylum.

Eduard Hitzig studied at Friedrich-Wilhelms University in Berlin and Julius-Maximilians University in Würzburg, learning from notable figures like Emil Du Bois-Reymond, Rudolf Virchow, Moritz Heinrich Romberg, and Carl Friedrich Otto Westphal. He was a member of the Nassovia Würzburg Corps (1859) and the Neoborussia Berlin Corps (1860). He earned his medical doctorate in 1862 and started his medical career as an electrotherapist in Berlin. In 1872, he became qualified in internal medicine and psychiatry through habilitation in Berlin. By 1875, Hitzig became the director of the Burghölzli mental institution and a full professor of psychiatry at the University of Zurich. In 1879, he was appointed as the director of the Neuropsychiatric Clinic and a professor of psychiatry at the University of Halle, where he opened Prussia's first independent psychiatric and nerve clinic in 1891.

The Sense Poem Das Sinngedicht

The Sense Poem ("Das Sinngedicht" in German) is a novella cycle authored by Swiss poet Gottfried Keller. Its inception commenced in Berlin around 1851 when Keller conceived initial ideas, followed by the composition of introductory chapters in 1855. The major portion of the text, however, was crafted in Zurich during 1881, concomitant with its serialization in the "Deutsche Rundschau." A comprehensive edition was published at the year's close.

The cycle derives its name from an epigram, or "Sinngedicht," by Baroque poet Friedrich von Logau, a work that assumes significance within the cycle. The epigram, "Wie willst du weiße Lilien zu roten Rosen machen? / Küß eine weiße Galathee: sie wird errötend lachen!" alludes to Galateia, the embodiment of female beauty's dual nature—provocative allure and tempering influence. Logau's composition serves as a poetic discourse on gallant advice. The cycle's seven novellas are entwined within a framing narrative—a love story set in the romantic environs of a 19th-century German university town. The protagonist, Herr Reinhart, a young naturalist, engages in a spirited exchange with Lucie, a hostess of wit and beauty. Through the exchange of Logau's epigram, they embark on a discussion revolving around the equality of genders in fostering successful marriages, evoking tales exemplifying diverse love choices. The narrative culminates in Reinhart and Lucie's burgeoning affection.

Keller's "Das Sinngedicht" garnered substantial acclaim among contemporary readers and literary critics, becoming a pinnacle of his literary career. Its success was underscored by successive editions, with reviewers likening the work's stature to that of Boccaccio's "Decameron." Literary historians lauded its intricate interplay of framing narrative and embedded tales. However, the work's accessibility waned in the 20th century due to evolving literary tastes. Rediscovery in the 1960s illuminated the cycle's multilayered engagement with themes spanning gender relations, the interplay of natural and intellectual sciences, and societal change. "Das Sinngedicht" demands nuanced interpretation due to its thematic complexity. Keller's innovative structuring, including chapter titles reminiscent of Cervantes' "Don Quijote," imbues the work with a playful-ironic ambiance. The male protagonist's perspective shapes the framing narrative, analogous to Cervantes' Don Quijote, contributing to the novella cycle's narrative charm.

The Diary and the Dreambook (Das Tagebuch und das Traumbuch)

In 1838, when he was barely 20 years old, Heller stated that he felt that the independence of anyone who did not keep a diary was threatened, because "... this independence can only be preserved by constant reflection on oneself, and this is best done by keeping a diary". The poet himself did not adhere to this maxim for the rest of his life- in 1843, he kept a short diary that gives a deeper insight into the poet's life and work.

In the Dream Book, which he kept from 1846, he recorded his dreams but also reflected on political events such as the revolutionary year of 1848.

The People of Seldwyla (Die Leute von Seldwyla)

The People of Seldwyla (Die Leute von Seldwyla) is a two-part novella cycle. The first five novellas, Part I, were written by Keller between 1853 and 1855 in Berlin, and they were published in 1856 by the Vieweg Verlag. The subsequent five novellas, Part II, were composed in several stages between 1860 and 1875, primarily during Keller's tenure as State Secretary in Zurich. The complete work was published between 1873 and 1875 by Göschen'sche Verlagsbuchhandlung. It comprises ten "life portraits" (the working title during the Berlin phase), interconnected by a shared setting—the fictional Swiss town of Seldwyla. With the exception of "Romeo und Julia auf dem Dorfe," an adaptation of Shakespeare's tragedy, the Seldwyla stories are comedies in novella form, characterized by a strong satirical and grotesque element. "Die Leute von Seldwyla" is regarded as a masterpiece of 19th-century German narrative art and is representative of the poetic realism style. Two of the novellas, "Romeo und Julia auf dem Dorfe" and "Kleider machen Leute," hold a place in world literature and are among the most widely read narratives in German-language literature. They have been adapted into films and operas multiple times, translated into numerous languages, and are available in an extensive array of editions.

"The People of Seldwyla," stands as a masterpiece of realistic fiction. Through a series of intricately woven tales set in the fictional town of Seldwyla, Keller presents a vivid tapestry of human nature and societal dynamics. His characters, caught in the crosshairs of their desires and societal expectations, reflect Keller's astute observations of the human condition within a changing world. With its rich character studies, social commentary, and timeless themes, this collection resonates as an emblem of literary realism and remains a cornerstone of Swiss literature.

Part I

Pankraz, the Schmoller
Romeo and Juliet in the village
Frau Regel Amrain and her youngest
The Three Righteous Comb Makers (Die drei gerechten Kammacher)
Mirror, the kitten (Spiegel das Kätzchen)

Part II
Clothes Make the Man (Kleider machen Leute)
The Blacksmith of his Fortune (Der Schmied seines Glückes)
The Lost Laughter
The Abused Love Letters (Die mißbrauchten Liebesbriefe)
Dietegen

Martin Salander

"Martin Salander" is both the title of a family and historical novel by Gottfried Keller, published in 1886. This final work by the author is a candid critique of conditions in his own country and beyond. The idealistic but credulous and naive titular character returns to his Swiss homeland after a lengthy stay in Brazil, achieving prosperity as a merchant and engaging in political activities. However, he witnesses how the unchecked pursuit of social advancement leads many contemporaries into fraud and embezzlement, resulting in him and his family becoming victims of such schemes. His hope that people, endowed with political rights in their country, would interact more responsibly with each other is bitterly disappointed, leading him to hand over the management of his business to his pragmatic son by the novel's end.

In his later work, Gottfried Keller undertook an experiment on multiple fronts. He engaged with contemporary history more directly than in any of his previous works and ventured into new formal pathways by attempting to minimize the use of an authoritative narrator. Despite varying reception, the novel held norm-setting power for many subsequent Swiss writers.

Seven Legends (Sieben Legenden)

The Seven Legends is a novella cycle initially published in 1872 but conceived during the author's time in Berlin. This slim work established Keller's reputation in Germany, although it sparked controversy. The Legends' centerpiece is the Virgin Mary, depicted in an interpretation and form divergent from both Catholic and Protestant perspectives. She assumes the role of the "magna mater of earthly and affectionate love," embodying a syncretic deity merging elements of Paganism and Christianity into a feminine trinity of love or a post-Christian Mother Earth. While Theodor Fontane found it repugnant for deviating from the natural simplicity of the legend form, Eduard Mörike was captivated by it. In this collection of allegorical tales, Keller delves into the realms of myth and spirituality.

Printed in Great Britain
by Amazon

58426881R00020